This Little Tiger book belongs to:

_____

_____

_____

For Jon, Evan and Colette – A B

LITTLE TIGER PRESS
1 The Coda Centre, 189 Munster Road, London SW6 6AW
www.littletiger.co.uk

First published in 2013
This edition published 2013

Text and illustrations copyright © Alison Brown 2013

Alison Brown has asserted her right to
be identified as the author and illustrator of this work
under the Copyright, Designs and Patents Act, 1988

A CIP catalogue record for this book is available
from the British Library

Eddie
and Dog

Alison Brown

LITTLE TIGER PRESS
London

Eddie dreamed of adventure.

He imagined flying to **far-off places** and doing **amazing things**.

Then one day . . .

. . . someone appeared, who was looking for adventure too. He walked up to Eddie. Eddie asked if he wanted to play.

He did.

Together they hunted for **crocodiles** . . . and sailed the **seven seas**.

They built a secret
fortress . . .

and explored a
faraway jungle.

But when they got home, Eddie's mum said the dog couldn't stay because they didn't have a garden. He would not be happy, stuck inside all day.

So he **had to go.**

Eddie couldn't stop thinking about him.

The dog must have thought about
Eddie, too. Because the next day . . .

he came back.

Eddie's mum couldn't believe it!
But she said they had to find him
a better home – one with a garden.

Eddie didn't think there was anything wrong with his home.

The dog must have thought the same.

Because three days later,

to Eddie's delight . . .

he came back.

Eddie's mum took the dog to stay in the country. She said he would be happy there.

Eddie didn't think so.

Eddie was alone again.

He wondered

if the

dog was

missing him

too.

Then, later that night,
Eddie heard a noise.

It was the dog.

He had come **back!**

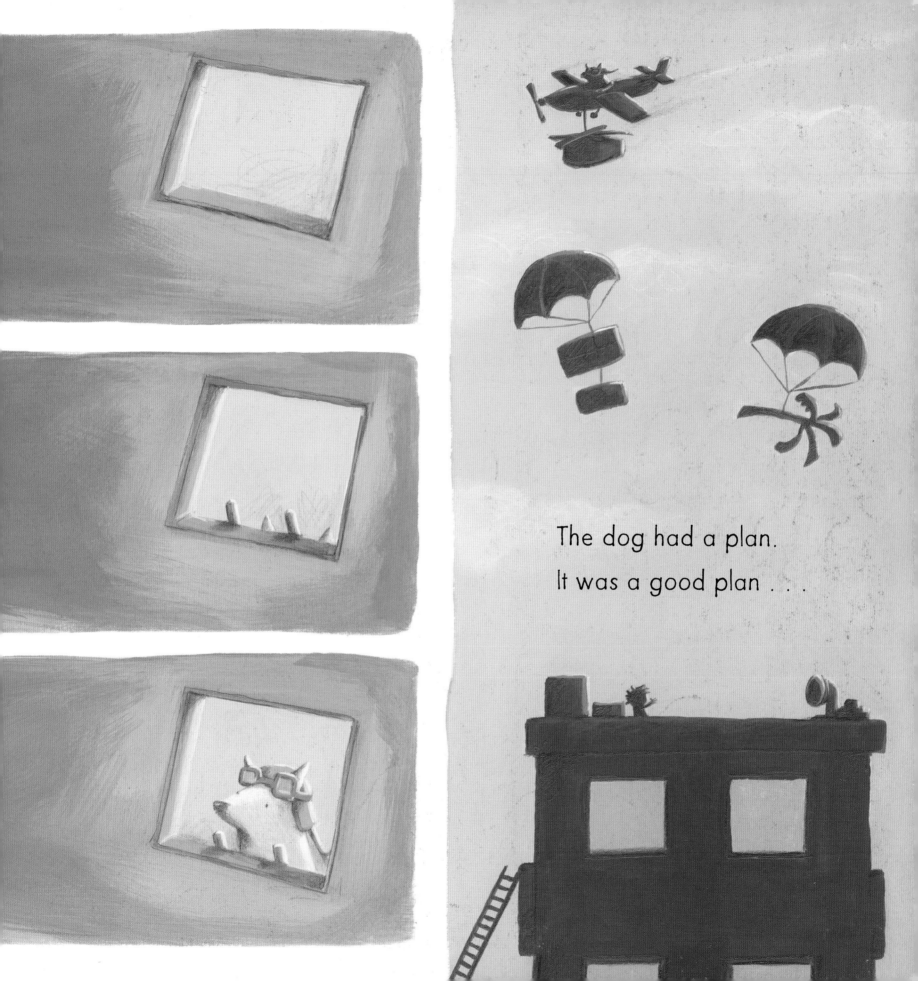

The dog had a plan.
It was a good plan . . .

. . . a garden on the roof!

Eddie's mum loved it. She
said the dog could live with
them. He'd be happy now.

Eddie was happy too.
His friend was here to stay . . .

. . . and it was time for adventure!

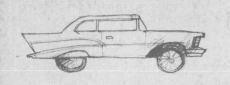

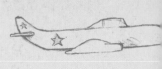
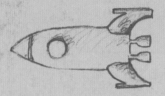

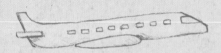

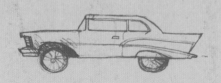

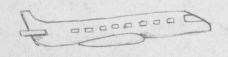

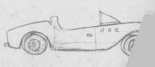

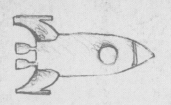
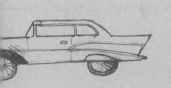

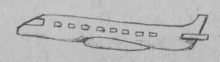
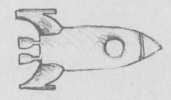
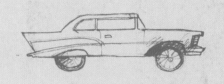
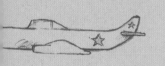
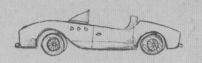

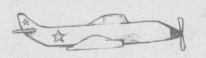

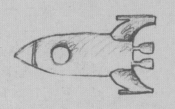
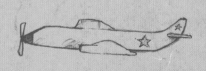

Super-Duper Dudley!
Sue Mongredien
Caroline Pedler

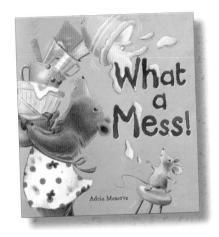

What a Mess!
Adria Meserve

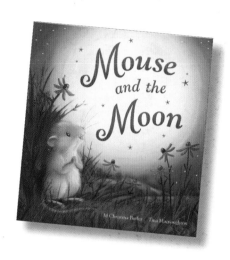

Mouse and the Moon
M Christina Butler · Tina Macnaughton

SUPER-PANTS!

More exciting adventures

from Little Tiger Press!

Star Friends
Tracey Corderoy
Alison Edgson

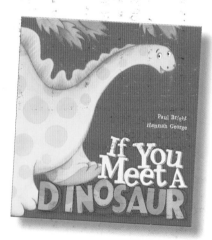

Paul Bright
Hannah George

IF You Meet A DINOSAUR

For information regarding any of the above titles or for our catalogue please contact us:
Little Tiger Press, 1 The Coda Centre, 189 Munster Road, London SW6 6AW
Tel: 020 7385 6333 • Fax: 020 7385 7333
E-mail: info@littletiger.co.uk • www.littletiger.co.uk